Published by
Armadillo Books
an imprint of
Bookmart Limited
Registered Number 2372865
Trading as Bookmart Limited
Blaby Road
Wigston
Leicester LE18 4SE

ISBN 1-84322-277-9

10 9 8 7 6 5 4 3 2 1

Produced for
Bookmart Limited by
Nicola Baxter
PO Box 215
Framingham Earl
Norwich NR14 7UR

Designer: Amanda Hawkes
Production designer: Amy Barton
Illustrator: Peter Glover/Advocate

Printed in China

Speed to read with the cheekiest car!

The car in this story is fast and fun, and your child's first steps in reading can be just the same when you share this book at home. It can be used in several ways to help beginning readers gain confidence.

You could start by reading the illustrated words at the edge of each lefthand page with your child. Have fun trying to spot the same words in the story itself.

All the words on the righthand page have already been met on the facing page. Help your child to read these by pointing out words and groups of words already met.

Finally, all the illustrated words can be found at the end of the book. Enjoy checking all the words you can both read!

Chase that Car!

Written by Nicola Baxter · Illustrated by Peter Glover

ARMADILLO

car

garage

man

keys

Mrs Mack wants a new car.

She goes to the garage. "I need a nice, safe car," she says. "I don't like to go fast."

"I have just the car for you," says the man at the garage.

"Perfect!" Mrs Mack smiles. "I do like this car. I'll call her Cleo."

The man hands Mrs Mack the keys to the car.

Cleo smiles. "I **do** like to go fast!"
she says.

road

Mrs Mack drives off down the road. Cleo speeds up.

"Slow down!" calls Mrs Mack. "Look out!"

Cleo goes faster.

lady

buggy

A lady with a buggy and a dog has to run.

Cleo just misses the dog.

"Help!" calls Mrs Mack. She is very frightened.

dog

Cleo goes faster and faster!

farmer

cow

gate

eyes

Mrs Mack sees something ahead.

"Slow down!" she shouts.

Cleo zooms on.

Mrs Mack can see a farmer.

She can see a cow.

She can see lots of cows coming through a gate onto the road!

"We're going to crash!" Mrs Mack shuts her eyes.

Cleo zooms through the gate.

field

Bump!

Bump!

Bump!

Cleo drives fast over a field!

steering wheel

Mrs Mack holds onto
the steering wheel.

"Wheee!" shouts Cleo.

"Aaaaah!" shouts Mrs Mack.

hill

hedge

Cleo goes up a hill
and down a hill
and through a hedge…
onto a new road.

"Wheee!" Cleo drives fast
up the new road.

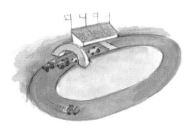

race track

racing car

flag

people

Oh no! It is not a road! It is a race track!

Cleo is so happy.
She can go as fast as she likes.

Poor Mrs Mack!

Zoom! Cleo passes
a yellow racing car.

Zoom! She passes
a blue car.

There is a man waving a flag.
People are cheering.

Cleo stops at last.

Mrs Mack is so happy!

cup

flowers

telephone

taxi

Mrs Mack and Cleo have won the race!

"Well done!" says a lady. She gives Mrs Mack a cup and some flowers.

"Oh … thank you," says Mrs Mack. "Do you have a telephone?"

Mrs Mack calls a taxi.

"But why not drive your car?" asks the lady.

"Oh no!" says Mrs Mack. "She can stay here!"

"Oh, thank you!" says Cleo.

truck

tractor

bicycle

snail

Mrs Mack goes back to the garage.

"I want my old car back, please," she says.

Soon Mrs Mack is driving home.
Her old car is very slow.

A truck passes her.

A tractor passes her.

A bicycle passes her.

A snail passes her, too!

Mrs Mack does not mind.
She is very happy.

The old car is very happy, too!

Picture dictionary

Now you can read these words!

bicycle

buggy

cow

cup

dog

eyes

farmer

field

flag

flowers

garage

gate

hedge

hill

keys

lady

man

people

race track

racing car

road

snail

steering wheel

taxi

telephone

tractor

truck